PHANTOM OF THE SEVEN STARS

Start Publishing PD LLC
Copyright © 2024 by Start Publishing PD LLC

Start Publishing PD is a registered trademark of Start Publishing PD LLC
Manufactured in the United States of America

Cover art: Shutterstock/Taisiya Kozorez

Cover design: Jennifer Do

10 9 8 7 6 5 4 3 2 1

ISBN 979-8-8809-0979-7

Phantom of the Seven Stars

by Ray Cummings

Lovely Brenda Carson, scholarly Jerome, pompous Livingston ... everyone aboard the Seven Stars scoffed at the idea of a Phantom Pirate. But I.P. agent Jim Fanning didn't laugh. He knew the luxury-liner's innocent looking cargo was already marked for plunder.

Part of my assignment on this space-flight of the *Seven Stars* was to watch the girl. That much, at least, wasn't hard. She was certainly easy to look at—a little beauty, slim with a pert, oval little face framed by unruly pale-gold hair. With mingled starlight and earthlight gleaming in that hair, it was like spun platinum. Her name was Brenda Carson. Certainly, she was an inspiring figure to any young man, in her white blouse and corded black and white trousers and her long black traveling cape with its hood dangling at the back of her neck and the cape folds flowing from her slim shoulders almost to the ground.

We were several days out from New York, with Mars, our destination, hanging like a great dull-red ball among the blazing stars in the black firmament ahead of us, when I first noticed that there was anything queer about Brenda. We were sitting under the glassite pressure-dome on the forepeak of the *Seven Stars*, bathed in the pallid starlight. By ship-routine it was mid-evening.

I gestured toward one of the side bull's-eyes of the bow-peak. "Gloomy-looking world, that Asteroid-9," I said.

The little asteroid, one of the many out here in the belt between the orbits of Earth and Mars, was a small leaden crescent of sunlight with the unlighted portion faintly putty-colored. It was, I knew, a world some five-hundred miles in diameter, amazingly dense so that its gravity was not a great deal less than Earth. A bleak, barren little globe. It had an atmosphere breathable for humans; there was water—occasional rainfall; but chemicals in the cloud-vapors poisoned the water for human consumption. The rocks were heavily laden with metals. But they were all base metals, of no particular value. So far as I knew, nobody had ever bothered to settle on Asteroid-9. It was completely uninhabited.

"Asteroid-9?" Brenda murmured. "Is that what it's called?"

Something in my chance remark had frightened her. Her blue eyes as she flung me a quick, startled glance were suddenly clouded with what might have been terror.

Her brother Philip was with us. He quickly said, "Asteroid-9? Somebody said we pass pretty close to it this voyage." He laughed. "Rotten sort of place, by what I've heard. You can have it and welcome."

I must explain that I was—and still am—an IP Man. My name, Jim Fanning. I was assigned as Lieutenant to Patrolship two. I had been on vacation, in New York. My ship, one of the biggest in the Interplanetary Patrol, was now on roving duty somewhere in the vicinity of Mars. Then suddenly an emergency with the *Seven Stars* had arisen. Chief Rankin had planted me on her. Only the captain knew my identity. To the dozen or so passengers, I was merely a young civilian traveler.

"I've never been to Asteroid-9," I was saying. And I, too, laughed casually, "I agree with you, Carson. Nice place to die in, but I guess that's all."

There was no question but what Brenda was trying to hide her sudden emotion. Terror? Was that it? We said no more about the asteroid; chatted of other things, and we were presently joined by another of the passengers.

"Ah, beautiful night," he greeted us. "I never get tired of the glories of the starways. Good evening, Miss Carson." He nodded smilingly to Philip Carson and me, and drew up a chair with us. His name was Arthur Jerome, well-known to me, though I had never before met him. He was a big, florid, distinguished-looking man of forty-odd; a habitual Interplanetary traveler, who between flights lectured over the earth television networks on things astronomical.

We talked for a while, and then suddenly Arthur Jerome said, "Nobody mentions the Phantom bandit. You know, if anything could spoil my interest in Interplanetary travel, it's to have a weird thing like that come up."

"Phantom bandit?" Brenda Carson murmured. "Is there—is there really such a thing?"

Arthur Jerome shrugged. "Naturally it's had no publicity. But things get out. Those last three accidents to space-liners—you can't hide that sort of thing. And you wouldn't call it supernatural. Or would you?"

*

The Phantom of the starways! That was the crux of my being here on the *Seven Stars*. Weird, mysterious thing—no wonder the Earth, Mars and Venus governments had not dared let it get any publicity which they could possibly avoid. For three months now, this Earth-year of 2170, mysterious accidents had been happening to commercial space-ships. Non-arrival at destination, and then later found by the Interplanetary Patrol, derelicts in space. Gruesome damn' thing. A ship unharmed, save that its air was gone. As though some mysterious accident had broken one of the pressure valves, or deranged the machinery of an exit-porte, so that the air had all hissed out. Ship of the dead. Everyone aboard lying asphyxiated.

It was eerie.

A "ghost-vessel" attacking the liners? A modern version of the ancient *Flying Dutchman* legend? Radio newscasters talked of things like that. A vengeful ghost-ship roaming the starways, with dead pirates aboard, bent on attacking the living navigators whom they hated just because they were alive. It made nice gruesome broadcasting to give the television audience the shivers. Supernatural legends easily get support. Particularly from hysterical, imaginative women, or cranks who crave publicity. Reports had come from amateur astronomers who owned fairly decent telescopes that they had seen the wraith of a pallid ghost-ship hovering up in Earth's stratosphere; passengers on liners had hysterically thought they saw the same thing.

A supernatural menace. But no reputable observer had ever seen anything. Our Interplanetary Patrol was completely baffled. And what the public didn't know was that those wrecked vessels—one of them, at least—had shown evidence that it had been hit by an electronic space-gun with a range of several hundred miles, which had broken the pressure-dome and let the air out. And in every case the wrecked ship was looted; the passengers' money and jewelry gone; the Purser's safe rifled.

"Anyway, it's a good thing for us," Arthur Jerome was saying, "the little *Seven Stars* ought not to be much of a prize for the phantom raider." He grinned, with his hand ruffling his sandy hair. "Let's hope we escape."

The *Seven Stars* not much of a prize? It was certainly reasonable enough to think that. We had a few Martians in the second-class section, and a few Earthmen passengers; and just an average commercial cargo. That's what anyone would think; and only the captain and I knew differently. Our cargo was anything but average. The boxes, as they had come aboard and been stored in the hold, were labeled as American preserved food-stuffs; technical commercial instruments, German-made prisms, lenses and the like. But in reality those boxes were crammed only with modern electronic weapons of war. It was a shipment purchased by the Martian government which was faced by the insurrection of its wealthy colony on Deimos. They were unusual weapons of exclusive Earth-manufacture. Small, for short-range, hand-use only; weapons to disable, but not injure. The recently publicized so-called "paralysis gun" was one of them. The Martian government, humane at least in battle with its own people, desperately needed this type of weapon in its forthcoming invasion of Deimos to subdue the rebels.

*

Not much of a prize, our little commercial liner *Seven Stars* this voyage? Just the opposite! Those rich colonists of Deimos most certainly would pay well to keep this shipment away for Mars! Would news of it have leaked out? Would the Phantom of the Starways attack the *Seven Stars* for just that purpose? Chief Rankin, of the Interplanetary Patrol, certainly thought it a possibility. He had put me aboard here; and as only the Captain and I knew, my ship—Patrolship-2—had been ordered to join us out here somewhere and convoy us to Mars. Convoy us against an attack by an enemy that you couldn't see!

"The Phantom raider!" Young Philip Carson was echoing Arthur Jerome's lugubrious words. "You suppose there is really any such thing?" I saw him exchange a glance with his sister. He laughed, but it wasn't much of a success.

"I doubt it," I agreed. "So far as I ever heard, those accidents were—well, just accidents. An air-valve can go wrong, you know, and dump the air out of a ship. Air goes quickly, and with a pretty powerful rush, if it once gets started.... Gruesome kind of talk, Miss Carson," I added lightly.

She tried to smile. My heart went out to her in that moment. Her beauty, I suppose; but somehow she seemed horribly pathetic. That mention of Asteroid-9 mysteriously frightened her; and now this mention of the phantom spaceship terrified her even more.

"You're right," Arthur Jerome agreed. "The supernatural is fascinating. Or a thing that you can't see but still can kill you—that's just as gruesome."

"And fascinating?" Philip Carson put in sourly. "Well, it may be to you, but it's frightening my sister. Let's talk of something else."

Then another passenger joined us. That girl was a magnet to men.

"Well, well, Miss Carson," he boomed as he came up. "You are looking very beautiful in the starlight." He sat down with us. His name was Walter J. Livingston—the Very Honorable Walter J. Livingston to give him his official title. He had just been appointed by the President of the World-Federation as Earth Ambassador to the Martian Government; was on his way there now to present his credentials. He was a big, heavy-set fellow, with a mass of iron-gray hair, a ribbon across his ruffled shirt-bosom; and the out-jutting jaw and booming voice of a born politician. Did he by any chance know the contents of the *Seven Stars'* cargo, this voyage? So far as I had been informed, he did not. I studied him now, and instinctively I didn't like him—possibly because of the extravagant compliments he was paying Brenda Carson.

The talk went on, and presently as I glanced up to the little control tower under the pressure-dome above us, I saw the bulky figure of Captain Wilkes standing there. He caught my gaze and furtively gestured. I excused myself in a moment; sauntered down the narrow side deck, turned a distant corner of the little superstructure. Then I went up to its roof, and forward again. In a moment I was in the control tower.

*

Captain Wilkes was there, seated alone with his electro-telescope beside him. He slid the oval doors closed upon us.

"Your ship's in sight," he greeted me. "Thought you'd be interested."

Patrolship-2, coming to convoy us. I took a look through the eye-piece of the telescope. Familiar vessel on which I had spent so many months. Its long cylindrical alumite hull, with the pressure-dome over its single upper deck, was painted by sunlight on one side and starlight on the other as it headed diagonally toward us. By the range-finder on the telescope I measured its visual length.

"Ten thousand miles off us," I said to the captain.

"Yes. Just about. Now listen, Fanning—there'll be no contact. It will circle us, close at hand. If the passengers ask you why we need any convoy—we don't want any panic here you know."

What he had in mind about explaining this convoy was never disclosed. He was staring through a duplicate eye-piece, and suddenly his words were checked as he sucked in his breath.

"Good Lord, Fanning—"

I saw it also—a tiny puff of electronic light at the top of the oncoming patrolship's dome. There was nothing else to be seen, I searched the starfield in that second of premonitory horror. Absolutely nothing visible. Just that puff of light where an electronic shot must have struck.

"Fanning—you saw that?" Captain Wilkes murmured.

"Yes."

Another few seconds. It seemed an eternity. And then the Patrolship wavered; drunkenly lurching and slowly turning over! Ghastly silent drama, out there in space ten thousand miles away. We could not see its details; just the tiny image of the ship, lurching, turning end over end.

A derelict in space. My horrified imagination pictured the air hissing out, spewing wreckage and bodies out perhaps. Ship of the dead, all in those seconds. Then it was hanging poised, slowly turning on a drunken axis of its own. The leprous, smashed dome was for a moment visible as it turned.

The Phantom raider had struck again!

*

My comrades. Thirty of them meeting their deaths out there in that moment. The thought numbed me. Captain Wilkes had leaped to his feet.

"Why—why, good Lord, it got them! And now—us next!"

Our convoy gone. Unquestionably that was because the phantom was after us!

"What are you going to do?" I murmured. "Not tell the passengers—"

"Good Lord, no. Nor the crew. What good would it do? We're not armed with long-range guns—no preparations to make. Only spread panic maybe among my men. Some of them might want to try and persuade me to turn back to Earth."

"And you're not going to do that?"

"Hell, no." Captain Wilkes was a choleric fellow. His ham-like fist crashed down on his desk. "I was told to run this cargo to Mars, and by Heaven, Fanning, that's what I'm going to do. Make a run for it." He swung for his controls. "I can use a greater Earth-repulsion and once we get past Asteroid-9, by a little jockeying I can use that, too. We'll see if there's any damn' phantom-ship going to overtake us."

It was a weird, gruesome feeling, realization that in all probability we were being pursued by something we couldn't see. Something still ten thousand miles away. Could it overtake us? Certainly not in less than a few hours, perhaps not even in a day. And then, would there be a flash of an electronic space-gun, weirdly from its unseen source? The crash of our hull, or our pressure-dome exploding outward; the wild rush and hiss of our air out into the vacuum of space? And then death by suffocation all in a minute or two.

The thing had me shuddering. I must have been murmuring something of my thoughts, for Captain Wilkes retorted:

"If they crash us with a shot they might very easily injure the cargo. More apt to try running in close to us—a boarding party with powered pressure-suits." His fist thumped his desk again. "An' by Heaven, if they try that—you got a gun, Fanning?"

"Yes," I agreed. I had a small weapon of the paralyzer-gun type, efficient at a few feet of range. But of what use against an enemy you couldn't see?

Wilkes presently dismissed me. "You keep your own counsel," he told me. He lowered his voice. "By what your Chief Rankin intimated, there's at least a reasonable possibility that we've some damn' spy on board."

"Well, if that's a fact," I said, "the Phantom won't try cracking us with a long-range gun and killing the spy as well as the rest of us."

"Exactly. That's what I'm counting on. Keep your eyes open and your ears stretched. Report to me anything that looks queer."

*

I left him presently. Dogged, indomitable old fellow. He was seated grimly at his desk with his astronomical charts as he figured by what ingenuity he could map an emergency course to give the little *Seven Stars* its greatest speed. The ship was silent as I padded the length of the superstructure roof and went down to the stern triangle. By ship-routine it was now about eleven at night. The Martian Passengers were out of sight, sleeping probably. None of the crew were about, save the man in the aft peak with his small, wide-angle telescope. The wreck of the patrolship was certainly far beyond sight of the naked eye. This stern lookout evidently hadn't spotted it, and in a moment now I knew it would be beyond his range also. The captain and I, doubtless, were the only ones who knew what had happened.

I went forward along the side deck. In the men's smoking lounge, amidships in the superstructure, I heard voices, caught a glimpse as I went past of Arthur Jerome, the television lecturer, and Livingston, the Earth Ambassador to Mars, in there with Green, the ship's purser. Did that mean that Brenda Carson and her brother were still on the forward peak? I went cautiously forward. They were there—the blobs of them, faintly starlit, showed where they were standing together at one of the side bull's-eyes. Upon impulse, instead of joining them, I slid unseen into the shadows of a loading engine.

"Oh, Philip—" The girl's voice was faintly audible in the silence. "I'm so frightened. You think we can do it safely?"

"Yes, of course. I'll make sure—" He lowered his voice and I lost the rest of it.

"When?" she murmured.

"I'll just take a look presently. We're not there yet—closer in a few hours."

What, in Heaven's name, could that mean? Were these two spies, planted here on the *Seven Stars* by the phantom-bandits? Were they discussing the attack which Captain Wilkes and I feared? Certainly it did not seem so. Young Philip Carson wasn't much older than his sister. Slim, handsome, rather effeminate-looking fellow, with a weak jaw and slack mouth. He wore black and white trousers, somewhat like hers. He and she seemed devoted to each other. Rankin had told me that Philip Carson had a bad record of gambling and bad companions. Was the girl entangled because of him?

My mind went back to the meager details which Rankin had given me. Brenda and Philip Carson came of a cultured and once-rich family in New York. Their father—their only close living relative—had been a research physicist. An eccentric old fellow; he had built a laboratory down on Long Island where, working in secret, he was laboriously experimenting on something. Two years ago the place had exploded. Presumably he had been killed. But in the wreckage his body had not been found; nor was there anything to give a clue as to what he had been doing there.

Had he been building the phantom space-raider? The thought was obvious now. Brenda and Philip had denied knowing, when the authorities had questioned them. And now they were going to Mars, on this of all voyages, and for no reason that they had been able to give. Was the vanished eccentric Professor Robert Carson the Phantom raider? My heart leaped as I heard another fragment from the girl.

"You think you got his message correctly?"

"Yes, of course I did."

"If we can do it safely—Oh, Phil—the location."

"I've got it all figured out, Bren," he insisted. "Even made a little map—got it in the wallet of my jacket."

That stiffened me. I could see the blob of him standing there with her. The folds of his hooded cape, like hers, fell almost to his feet. But his arm held the cape draped a little to one side. I could see his white shirt; he was wearing no jacket. It would be in his sleeping cubby then.

For a moment more I crouched in the shelter of the little loading engine; I caught a few more fragments, but they were not important.

*

A wallet in young Carson's cubby, with a map in it? I shifted silently backward, reached the side deck and padded aft. The smoking lounge was empty now. The little interior cross corridor of the superstructure was dim and silent. Carson and his sister had connecting rooms, with corridor doors side by side. Cautiously I tried them. They were locked.

In a moment I was out to the side deck. Carson's window was closed; I pulled at the vertical sash and it yielded, slid outward. The room was dim, with just a faint glow of the corridor light coming over the lattice-grille above the door.

I jumped over the sill; landed silently in the room. No need for any lengthy search; his jacket was here, folded on a chair. The wallet was in a pocket. Swiftly I riffled through it, came upon a folded square of notepaper. The map? I was opening it. By the dim sheen of reflected light I could see its penciled scrawl. And suddenly I was stricken by the sound of footsteps in the corridor outside. Someone coming. I jumped on the chair. Through the grille I could catch a glimpse of a cloaked figure coming along the corridor. Carson or the girl—in that second I could not tell which.

But at all events I had no desire to get caught here by either of them. I got back out the window just in time. Aft down the side deck there was the blob of a loitering figure, a big, bulky silhouette. It was Walter Livingston, the Earth-Mars Ambassador. The tip of his cigarette glowed in the dimness as he stood by one of the side bull's-eyes. Was he watching these windows of Carson and the girl? Did he see me? I had no way of telling. I ran forward, ducked around the superstructure corner. The bow-peak triangle was empty; the chairs where the group of us had been sitting were still here.

There was enough light for me to examine the folded sheet of paper I had purloined. It seemed a crude map. A rough, penciled sketch. But a map of what? There were the ragged outlines of what might be intended to represent mountains. The scribbled word: "Andros." A dotted line through what might be a mountain pass. And then a tiny X.

I stared at the thing, puzzled. A few hundred years ago the fabled surface-ship pirates of Earth's romantic sea-history supposedly made maps like this. Maps of buried treasure. Pirates' gold. Were Carson and his young sister after some treasure? Where? On Earth? Mars? Little Deimos? Asteroid-9? That thought leaped at me. Certainly they had shown a queer interest in my chance remark about Asteroid-9. We were not far from it now. Fifty thousand miles perhaps—would pass at our closest point to it in an hour of two. I stared through the bull's-eye beside me. It was down there, diagonally ahead of us—a full-round, putty-colored disk, with the configurations of its mountains and the turgid clouds of its atmosphere beginning to be visible.

But what could any of that have to do with the Phantom raider, or the attack on the patrolship and the impending attack upon us? Surely there was no treasure on Asteroid-9. The treasure, if you could call it that, was right here on board the little *Seven Stars*.

I was crouching now in the shadow of the loading engine on the bow-peak, puzzled by my rush of thoughts. Should I take this to Captain Wilkes? Vaguely I realized that perhaps I should, but something stopped me. My own instinctive feelings for Brenda Carson. She seemed somehow so pathetic. Surely she was no plotting murderess. Her brother—yes. But the girl—protecting someone she loved? Was her father really the Phantom raider? His invention an X-flyer endowed with mechanical, electronic invisibility? I knew that such a thing was scientifically possible, of course. But Professor Carson was a frail old man. And my mind leaped back to some other things Chief Rankin had told me. The Phantom was thought to be a notorious Earth-criminal who, a few years ago, had been known as the "Chameleon." A fellow skilled in the art of wax disguise so that none of the Earth crime-trackers really knew what he looked like. He was wanted in both Great New York and Great London for mail-tube murders. Nothing was known of his identity save that he had once had an operation for a fractured skull, where in the back of the skull a big triangular platinum plate had been inserted to take the place of the shattered bone. A criminal surgeon, dying, had confessed that much; had said he had performed the operation. And then he had mumbled something about the Chameleon being the Phantom raider.

Surely such a notorious skilled adventurer could not be old Professor Carson. I decided not to have Brenda and Philip hauled before the captain now for questioning.

*

Thoughts are instant things. I was crouching there behind the engine loader no more than a moment; and suddenly down the other side deck just beyond the smoking lounge, I saw a moving figure. A slight figure in dark cloak and hood—the bottoms of black and white trousers were visible. Brenda? It made my heart pound. For a second I stared as she ducked into a doorway. I was there in twenty seconds, until I saw the cloaked shadow of her going down a companion ladder into the ship's hold.

Swiftly I followed. Down two eight-foot levels, and then I caught another glimpse of her as she moved into the lower passage. It was a metal catwalk with small cubbies opening from it. The ship's air-renewers, ventilating system; a cubby controlling the hull gravity-plate shifters; other mechanism rooms. She went past them, a furtive little shadow. And stopped at what seemed the door to one of the tiny pressure chambers of an exit-porte in the side of the hull.

"Oh, you, Mr. Fanning? What do you want down here?" The voice in the silence so startled me that I whirled. It was Kellogg, the ship's gravity-control operator. In his shirtsleeves, pipe in hand, with a green eyeshade on his forehead, he had seen me from the door of his little cubby.

"Why—" I murmured. "Just coming down to see you." I turned to join him. And suddenly a buzzer in his control room interrupted him. I stood while he answered it—an audio-tube for direct voice-transmission.

"Yes, Captain Wilkes—" And then Kellogg gasped and clutched at the table beside him; then he whirled upon me, his face chalk-white. "Our radio-helio is smashed! Someone—something smashed it!"

16

Our little *Seven Stars* was cut off from Earth or Mars communication! Captain Wilkes had evidently decided to flash a call for help to Earth, and found that the apparatus had been smashed! But even that startling news instantly was stricken from Kellogg and me. Out in the corridor quite near us a low scream sounded! And then there was the sound of air hissing!

"What the devil!" Kellogg gasped.

My gun was in my hand as we ran. There was nothing in sight on the dim little catwalk. The scream had died. The air-hissing stopped.

"Somebody went into the pressure-chamber!" Kellogg muttered. "What in the hell—"

"The pressure-chamber door-slide was closed. I knew the mechanism of these exit-portes. There were four of them in the hull-bottom of the *Seven Stars*—two on each side. There was an inner door-slide; a sealed pressure-room some ten feet square and six feet high; and an outer door-slide. Ordinarily the mechanism was automatic. The outer slide must be closed if the inner one was open. To make an exit, one went into the pressure-room; closed the catwalk door, and with manual control slowly opened the outer slide, so that the air in the sealed room would hiss out into space. After which, with a thirty-second interval, the outer slide would close and the inner one slowly open, admitting the ship's air again into the pressure-room.

"Someone worked the manual controls wrong!" Kellogg was muttering. He gestured to where there was a duplicate set of controls out here in the corridor. "That outer slide opened too quickly!"

We could hear the last of the air rushing out with a wild gush. A stab of horror went into my heart. Brenda Carson in there, trying to escape from the ship—not knowing how to work the controls—opening that outer slide too quickly.

The air in the pressure-room was gone in a few seconds. Then we heard the click of the outer slide closing. The inner door began very slowly opening. With a muttered curse of impatience Kellogg twitched at the control levers here. The inner door slid wide.

We clutched at the catwalk rail to hold ourselves against the gust of wind as the little pressure-room filled. And then we rushed into it. Pressure suits, powered as I knew by tiny gravity-repulsers and a rocket-stream mechanism, stood here in racks. One of them lay here on the floor, entangled with a rack-post so that it had not blown out. Brenda evidently had tried to get into it and failed.

"Look! Good Lord—poor little thing—" Kellogg murmured. He had slid aside a tiny bull's-eye shade. Through it a segment of space outside the hull was visible.

We had only a glimpse of a ghastly body, mangled by the explosion of the pressure within itself, out in the pressureless vacuum of space. It floated past us, some forty feet out. Held poised by the gravity, the nearness and bulk of the *Seven Stars*. Horrible little satellite, already finding an orbit of its own, slowly circling around us.

*

I staggered back from the bull's-eye. As I rushed back along the catwalk my horrified mind was clamoring with the vague thought: had Brenda operated that pressure-mechanism wrongly? Or had someone on the catwalk, at the controls there, done it?

That thought, too, was stricken away. I reached the forward deck triangle. The bow-peak lookout was calling up to Captain Wilkes:

"Passenger overboard! Brenda Carson! It's Miss Brenda Carson!"

Dead girl in the space-light. I could not look at the horrible thing as it rounded our bow and came slowly floating past again.

"You, Fanning—what's happened? Brenda Carson, he says."

Arthur Jerome stood calling to me from his stateroom door at the bow superstructure corner. He was in his nightrobe with a negligee hastily wrapped around him.

"Yes—" I gasped. "Brenda Carson. She—"

"And I heard something about radio-helio room wrecked." The big, florid television lecturer seemed in a panic. Experienced space-traveler, but he had never run into anything like this before. I wouldn't blame him for his terror. But I had no time for him now. The ship was in confusion. I could hear the

Martians, below deck in the bow, shouting with frightened questions. Two or three members of the crew were running up to Captain Wilkes who was outside his turret calling down orders.

I ran down the side deck. One of the excited crew stopped me. "You seen young Philip Carson? Captain wants him."

I shook my head and ran on. Somebody else was calling Carson's name. I mounted the companionway to the superstructure roof. Had Philip Carson vanished? They couldn't find him? Well, what I knew about Philip Carson now I'd certainly tell Captain Wilkes! Suddenly I realized fully that because of Brenda I had wanted to keep silent—but there was no need of that now.

From the superstructure roof, as I ran forward along it, I could see down to the side deck. A cloaked figure there. Philip Carson. I had just a glimpse as he darted into a door under me. A ladder was nearby. My little paralyzer-gun was in my hand as I climbed down the ladder, reached the dark side-deck. The commotion was all up forward; there was no one here at the moment. The corridor door into which Carson had run was beside me. I ran into it, ten feet or so and into a cross corridor. Came to his doorway. It was locked. I ran around to the deck again. His window was near here.

The glassite pane of the window was closed and locked. The inner fabric-shade was drawn down. What was he doing in there? Searching for his map? For other things which might be incriminating?

I had a few instruments hidden in my clothes, tiny devices which we of the Interplanetary Patrol sometimes have occasion to use—a small electric listener and a tiny X-ray fluoroscope screen. The listener yielded the sound of a man's panting breath, his furtive, fumbling movements within the dark little cubby. Then I tried the X-ray, through the fabric-shrouded glassite pane of the window. It shot its invisible, soundless rays through the window into the cubby. The little hooded three-inch screen in my palm glowed with the greenish fluoroscopic X-ray image.

A kneeling skeleton was revealed—the skeleton of a man kneeling in there with his back to me. I stared, and suddenly gasped, with my breath stopped. The back of the skeleton's skull was visible—the image-shadow there was of a different density from the bones of his skull! A dark triangular patch—not bone, but metal! The man with the metal skull! Philip Carson, of notorious Chameleon fame! The Phantom raider! I had him here identified at last! Had him trapped here!

*

With a blow of my gun-butt I smashed through the glassite pane; tore the fabric-shade aside. This room was dark. I had an instant's glimpse of the dark blob of his crouching figure. There was the whiz of something he threw at me; the tinkling of glass as some fragile little thing struck against my forehead. I recall that my paralyzer ray darted into the dark room. Perhaps it caught him, held him for a second. But my head was reeling; my senses swiftly fading, with a cold sweat breaking out all over me.

And then I was aware that I had fallen to the deck with my gun clattering away. With my last dim thought came the realization that I was fainting. That tiny glass globe which had broken against my forehead—I knew what it was! A little bomb of acetycholine, a weird drug to lower the blood-pressure and cause me to faint. I fought, but it was useless. My senses faded.

Then after an interval I seemed vaguely to be conscious that someone was bending over me. A dark cloak.... Again I knew only blankness; and then slowly my senses were coming back. Weak, dizzy, with my head roaring, my body bathed in cold sweat, I found myself still lying on the dark deck. Perhaps I had been out only a moment or two. I could still hear the commotion up forward. I staggered to my feet; saw the cloaked figure as it ran into the superstructure. Carson making his getaway! I had a glimpse of him again, two levels down on the dim catwalk, and saw him dart into the pressure-chamber. I was too late getting there. The metal pressure-door closed in my face.

But I had him! I could do to him what he had done to Brenda! I started for the manual controls. I could open that outer slide, let the pressure-room air out with a rush before he could get into his space suit, blast him out into space, or suffocate him in the pressure-room.

But I had over-taxed my strength. My blood-pressure was still too low from that accursed drug. My senses were fading again and I sank to the floor. Weakly I tried to call Kellogg. But he wasn't in his little nearby cubby now.

I did not quite lose consciousness this time. I heard the air slowly going out through the outside opening slide. Then heard the click as the automatic mechanism closed it. The corridor slide in another moment, automatically was slowly opening. The rush of air into the little room helped revive me. I got to my feet again; ran into the room. I could see the empty space on the rack where he had taken one of the powered pressure suits and escaped. At the bull's-eye observation porte I had a glimpse of him—a bloated figure in his air-filled suit—a tiny comet with a radiance of rocket-stream like a tail behind it.

The blob of him in a moment had vanished. Where did he expect to go? Diagonally ahead, and far down in the glittering starfield, the round, putty-colored disk of Asteroid-9 was visible.

My strength had almost fully come back to me now. Quickly I got into another of the power-suits. They were a somewhat old-fashioned model, but adequate enough, a double-shelled fabric with electronic pressure-absorbing current in it; air-renewers, and the small power-units. I bloated the suit in another moment; closed the corridor slide. I let the air rush out through the outer slide as quickly as I dared.

And then I catapulted out, not bothering with the rocket-stream but using full gravity-repulsion against the bulk of the *Seven Stars*. Far down, ahead of me, for an instant I could just see the speck which was the fleeing Carson. Over me the bulk of the *Seven Stars* hung, a great alumite cylinder, receding, dwindled by distance until it was only a tiny speck, lost among the blazing stars.

With the huge, dull-lead disk of Asteroid-9 growing in visual size under me, I hurtled downward, using the asteroid's full attraction now as I sped after the escaping Carson.

*

Alone in space; a little drifting world of yourself. It is an eerie feeling. I have no idea how long that descent to Asteroid-9 took; one loses all sense of time as well as space, hurtling alone through the starry universe. The *Seven Stars* long since was gone, vanished in the black illimitable distances of the blazing firmament above me. Head down, with full attraction in the little gravity plates of the padded shoulders of my bloated suit, like a diver I headed, hurtling for the dull-lead surface.

I had picked up velocity swiftly. The great round disk of Asteroid-9 widened, spread, crawled outward and seemed visually coming up. For a time, sunlight was a thin stream on its distant curving limb of mountains. Then I went into the cone of its shadow. At once the look of the weird leaden mountains changed; starlight and earthlight mellow with a faint sheen that struck down through the clouds and tinged the giant ragged peaks with a tinting glow.

The clouds, still far down, were broken in thin stratas here over this hemisphere. The disk had widened now so that presently it filled all the lower half of the firmament; and a visual convexity had come to it. I tried to calculate my velocity by the apparent enlarging of the desolate scene as it rushed up at me.

Where was Carson? Long since, I had lost sight of the tiny speck which had been he. Was I overtaking him? I could not tell. With the leaden glow of the asteroid's surface as a background, I knew I could be quite close to him and still not see him. Undoubtedly he was not using his rocket-stream now; had only used it in starting, for quick repulsion against the ship's hull. I was sure he could not be very far below me unless, during the time which had passed, he had headed in some other direction, departing from a straight, swift descent. Could he drop faster than I was dropping? I doubted it. Unless he was very skilled—or very desperate, holding the asteroid's attraction to a dangerous point. I held my own until I dared hold it no longer. I was in the upper atmosphere now. In every direction, save above me, the planet's dark surface spread out to its jagged, circular horizon.

Then at last I dared not hold the attraction longer. With all the tiny plates in my suit electronized to full repulsion, I began slackening my fall. Still I had not glimpsed Carson. Disappointment was within me. What a long chance was this! A five-hundred-mile hemisphere of utter desolation. No food; no water. And I had no weapons or instruments, save the single little paralyzer-gun which I had snatched from the deck when I recovered my senses. I was beginning to be sorry now that I had so hastily left the *Seven Stars*. No chance of getting back; the die was cast, here on little Asteroid-9 pitted against this resourceful, youthful astonishing Interplanetary murderer.

What was Carson's plan? Escape from the ship had been a desperate necessity for him, of course. And my memory was back to the fragments I had heard between him and Brenda. I could understand them better now! They had planned from the beginning to escape to Asteroid-9! And poor little Brenda, entangled in this criminality with her brother, had left the ship first, and met her death. Memory of the map they had had came suddenly to me. I had it in my pocket now; I tried to conjure what it had looked like. Outlines of mountains; the word Andros. Was that the name of one of the asteroid's mountain peaks? Probably it was. I cursed myself for my ignorance. The Phantom raider probably was based upon this desolate asteroid. A hideout here, with food and water and possibly with some of the raiders' men living here. And Carson was dropping now to join them.

What chance had I against a layout like that?

But I had no choice now but hurtle downward, trying to check my descent as best I could. For a time, as I came out from under the clouds, with the dark, fantastic surface of naked, ragged little peaks no more than twenty or thirty thousand feet down, it seemed that I had been too brash; I was dropping too fast; never would I be able to check it. I would crash....

*

But that, too, was an error, born of my momentarily despairing thoughts. I was presently poised, some ten thousand feet up. The highest of the little peaks was no more than half that. They stood in a tumbled mass—jagged needle-spires—rocks and buttes and great round-top boulders, with ravines and gullies between them. Scene of utter, naked desolation, convulsed landscape, frozen into immobility.

And suddenly my heart was pounding with abrupt exultation. Far down, where the starlight and Earthlight bathed a little peak, I saw the speck which was the descending Carson! Just for a second the tiny outline of his bloated suit was clear against the background of a shining rock. Then he dropped into an inky shadow and was gone again.

I tried to mark the spot. A little triplet of spires, standing like sentinels above a small dark valley. Was that Andros, a landmark here? Probably it was.

I was down in perhaps another half hour, with the triplet of spires standing up against what was now a sullen sky of broken leaden clouds through which the starlight and Earthlight fitfully shone. I had landed, by all that I could judge, about half an Earth-mile from where Carson had dropped. Had he seen me coming down above him? Perhaps. Perhaps not.

With my helmet off, and with my lungs panting as they tried to adjust themselves to the weird air, I crouched for a moment in the shadow of a rock, peering, listening. There was nothing. It seemed a dead world, myself its only inhabitant—a silence so utter that my own breath, my pounding heart were roaring in my ears.

I started in a moment, heading along a ridged, fantastic little terrain at the bottom of a shadowed valley. The deflated suit hung in baggy folds upon me; the bulky helmet was folded, hanging down from the back of my neck. Half a mile to where Carson had dropped. Gun in hand I advanced as cautiously as I could, until presently I was following a ragged ditch with the triple spires of Andros looming above me.

Was this where Carson had landed? So far as I could judge, it seemed so. I was tense, alert with the vague, horrible feeling that I was walking into ambush.

Then ahead of me, in a distant shadow, it seemed that there was a faint stir of movement. Soundlessly I melted down to the lead-gray rocks. I could not see the shadow now, but every instant I expected the luminous darkness to be stabbed with a bursting bolt. There was nothing.

Suddenly the stillness was broken by a faint scraping sound. It seemed fairly close, and into the darkness from whence it had come I aimed my ray; pressed its lever.

There was a faint, gasping scream; then a choked silence. I jumped to my feet, holding the paralyzer-gun leveled as it throbbed and quivered in my grip. Got him! He couldn't move. He was rooted there in the darkness, with rigid, stiffened muscles as the ray held him.

I saw him in an instant, the dark blob of him almost merged with the shadows, with his baggy space-suit like my own deflated in folds upon him, and his helmet folded back.

Triumphant, I dashed forward; and then stopped transfixed, amazed. The paralyzed figure, stricken upright here on the rocks wasn't young Carson! Above the folded helmet there was a head of bobbed blonde hair! Brenda! Brenda, not dead! Not that ghastly thing that was a gruesome little satellite of the *Seven Stars*!

I saw her rigid face, with goggling mouth and staring eyes. Brenda mute, stricken by my ray. I snapped it off frantically; called to her as I dashed up. And as the ray released her, I saw her waver; then, with her knees buckling, she sank into a little heap on the ground.

If only I had some water to dash into her face! Frantically I knelt, holding her head, brushing her curls from her damp forehead. The ray, I knew, upon her for so short a time, should not quite do this to her. It was her emotion, her terror which had caused her to faint.

My mind went back to that hooded figure, cloaked, which I had chased in the ship's corridor. I had had a vague indecision, then had decided it was Brenda—and the ship's lookout at the bow-peak had confirmed my fears. But that had been Philip, and it was Brenda whom I had chased that second time, following her out the porte, hurtling into space after her.

"Brenda—"

She opened her eyes presently, bewildered, but she was unharmed.

"Oh—you—I was so frightened."

*

I held her as she recovered, and presently she was filling in all the grim details of her tragic little story. Whatever her brother Philip's propensities for gambling and bad companions, he had been no criminal. They had lost their father; had been truthful when they said they did not know what Professor Carson had been building in his lonely little laboratory. But they knew enough so that when the Phantom bandit began his mysterious raids, they suspected it was their father's ship; the laboratory explosion merely a blind. He had often mentioned, when they were children, that the dream of his life was to discover and perfect electronic invisibility.

"Albert Einstein of two hundred years ago," she was telling me now. "Father studied his writings and his theories very closely. He said that the secret of practical mechanical invisibility was clearly forecast by Einstein's discoveries."

"And you think now," I murmured, "your father is this mysterious Phantom raider?"

Her little face clouded. Her blue eyes, misty with Earthlight which was striking down upon us now through the clouds, gazed at me with a pathetic appeal.

"We did not know. We—we were afraid so. And then Philip got a message one night—"

Weird occurrence. Young Carson had been on the porch of their Long Island home. From the sky overhead, where nothing was to be seen, had come a little stab of waving white light. A helio signal. From their father? Certainly it seemed so. It told them to come secretly to Asteroid-9. He would be there, at the base of Andros. And so they had come to try and help their father.

"Help him?" I murmured.

"Yes. Oh, Mr. Fanning—"

"Jim is shorter," I interjected.

"—Jim, you see, we couldn't believe father is a criminal. Captured maybe and forced to operate his ship by these bandits, and appealing to us for help."

Desperate adventure indeed. But they had tackled it; had taken passage on the little *Seven Stars* which they understood would pass very close to Asteroid-9, this voyage. And they had known completely nothing of the *Seven*

Stars' cargo or of any plot which the raider might have against her! Brenda gasped now when I told her of those angles.

And there were still other angles that puzzled me. "Brenda, have you ever heard of an Earth-criminal called the Chameleon?"

She had not; and when I described his exploits of a few years ago, she was convinced that by no possible chance could her aged father have been secretly doing things like that. Nor Philip either, for that matter. She declared it vehemently, and I believed her. But the man with the metal skull had been on the *Seven Stars* as stowaway, or spy among the passengers, ship's officers or crew. I had seen him there in young Carson's stateroom.

Brenda, when I was chasing her, had eluded me. "I saw you fighting with somebody at Philip's window," she told me now. "I was going to escape from the ship then."

"Even though Philip was dead, you were going on with your plans alone?"

"Yes, why not?" She smiled her twisted little smile. "Then I saw you fall to the deck. I ran, bent over you. I—I thought you were dead. So I—I ran down to the porte and took off. Philip and I had planned it so carefully. Oh, poor Philip!"

"He didn't miscalculate those air-mechanisms," I muttered. "That damned villain must have been there in the corridor for an instant while I was talking to Kellogg, and shoved the controls—killed Philip."

And I had tried to do the same thing to Brenda! I could only thank the Lord now that I had failed!

*

The two of us, alone here on Asteroid-9. No food nor water. Perhaps the only inhabitants of this desolate little world.

Abruptly she was gripping me. "Look—Jim—look there!"

I followed her gesture. Up in the leaden sky beyond the looming triple spires of Andros, a tiny speck had appeared. A ship coming down. Breathlessly we watched. In a few minutes it was a little oblong blob.

"It's coming this way, Brenda."

"Yes."

It seemed circling a little. By the look it would land on a small level plateau some quarter of a mile from us. We stared, mute, transfixed, watching.

And then suddenly I sucked in my breath with a new shock of startled amazement. There was something familiar about that cylindrical alumite hull with the curving pressure-dome above it, and those quadruplicate tail-fins.

It wasn't the bandit flyer! "That's the *Seven Stars*!" I gasped.

The *Seven Stars* unquestionably. We saw her clearly in a moment, as she circled some five miles away from us and headed slowly for the small plateau. Captain Wilkes undoubtedly had changed his mind about trying to make a run for it. With chaos on his ship—his radio-helio wrecked so that he could not summon another convoy—he had headed down here to hide his vessel. And he did not know, of course, that the Phantom raider's base was here! He had brought his little treasure ship into the very camp of the enemy!

"We must warn him, Brenda."

The blob of the little liner dropped from our sight behind a line of broken rock-spires as she settled to the plateau. But we could tell within a few hundred yards of where she had landed. It took us only a few minutes to run there, with the slighter gravity of Asteroid-9 aiding us in our leaps across the intervening little chasms. And then we saw the *Seven Stars*, where she rested placidly on the level surface. One of her lower portes was open, but there were no figures out on the dim rocks.

There was silence inside as we entered the dark little pressure-chamber. As always customary in port, both its outer and inner door-slides were open, admitting the fresh outer air.

There was no one to greet us on the lower level catwalk. Its single overhead light was burning. We passed Kellogg's little cubby. No one was in it. Then we mounted the companion ladder; came to the superstructure corridor.

Queer, this silence. I held Brenda, with my heart chilling, sinking. It seemed suddenly that we were prowling like ghouls. The ship was so cold, so silent. With the ventilating fans stilled, the interior air here was turning fetid. I had an impulse to call out. Captain Wilkes, Controlman Kellogg, Purser Green, the crew, the passengers—where were they all? But abruptly I was furtive, with a slow, horrified terror dawning in me so that in the dim corridor I stood suddenly and turned to Brenda.

"We'd better get back out of here," I murmured. "Something queer—"

"Jim—look!"

We stood frozen, transfixed. At the deck doorway a blob was lying. Captain Wilkes. Dead—suffocated. I swept Brenda away that she might not get a second glimpse of his puffed, mangled flesh where it had burst outward from its own pressure. There had been a vacuum here! Out in space the little *Seven Stars* quite evidently had lost her interior air!

Ship of the dead! I took only one look at the dimly starlit deck triangle; the bodies lying strewn there. Little group of humans who had gathered there in a last frenzied panic, clinging to each other, falling one upon the other—suffocating, dying.

Nothing but the dead here.

But this tragedy had happened out in space! And we had seen the *Seven Stars* calmly coming down, gracefully, skilfully landing!

I swung back to Brenda. I gasped, "Good Lord, we've got to get out!"

Too late a realization! I was aware suddenly of a dark glistening shape behind us in the corridor—a man in a sleek tight-fitting black robe. His white face, evil with a leer, grinned at us. Brenda screamed. I tried to defend us from another dark blob that leaped from a doorway beside me. And then something struck my head. I was aware only that Brenda was screaming as I felt myself falling, my senses hurtling off into the soundless abyss of unconsciousness.

*

I came at last into a dim half-consciousness in which I realized that I was being carried. I could feel the rhythmic step; and then I knew that I was slung over a man's shoulder and that he was walking with me on the rocks. Other dark forms were beside us. With blurred vague vision I could see the little *Seven Stars* which we had left.

And near at hand another spaceship had landed now, here upon little Asteroid-9. I was being carried to it. I could glimpse it only vaguely as I hung inert on my captor's shoulder. It was a small ship, smaller than the *Seven Stars*, and of a type I had never seen before—barrel-finned and with a spreading fan-tail, somewhat in the British Earth-design. It rested on the rocks like a long, thin bird, with body puffed out underneath. Over it was the conventional glassite pressure dome, low-slung so that its top was no more than ten feet above the single deck. A dead-black bird. The starlight and mellow Earthlight were on it, but the black metal surface did not shimmer.

My senses wafted away again into another blank interval.... And then dimly my hearing came....

"We're glad to have you, little Brenda. You are a treasure indeed. A woman among us—to cook and sew with woman's duties. Your father will appreciate that. You do, eh Carson?"

Familiar, suave, ironic voice with a rich booming timber to it of assumed graciousness. I knew I had heard that voice before, but with my swimming senses now I could not quite place it. I felt my eyes opening to a blur of swaying outlines.

"You let her alone." The thin frightened voice of an old man. Brenda's father.

The dim scene clarified as my strength came. I was lying on the floor of a little circular control room, with a black shape beside me. And there were three other figures: Brenda, still garbed in her baggy deflated space-suit, with her white tense face staring in my direction; her gray-haired, thin father, in black trousers and black shirt, seated in a little metal chair beside her. And the other figure at the controls—a big, heavy-set man in tight-fitting black garment. Tubelight shone on his florid face. Arthur Jerome, Interplanetary traveler, Earth television lecturer on things astronomical! The man with the metal skull, unquestionably! Notorious chameleon of former years, and now the Phantom Raider!

"This Fanning comes to his senses," a voice beside me growled.

"Ah, so?" It brought Jerome with a leap, and then he bent over me. "So that blow on your head didn't kill you, Fanning?"

"No," I said. "You, Jerome. If only I had known—"

"Quite true," he chuckled. "Hindsight is very easy. And now we have you here. You will be useful, if you have any sense, A member of the Interplanetary Patrol, you should be skilled in many things of our adventuring in space. Romantic life, Fanning. Did you ever read of Captain Kidd, so long ago? One might say I am his modern incarnation. Romantic idea, eh Fanning?"

A little mad, this fellow. I could well imagine it. But a clever scheming, murderous villain for all that. "Much money for you," he added slyly. "I treat all my men well. There are fifteen of us here."

"I like money," I said with an assumption of sullenness. "But there are a lot of things I want to know."

I found that I was still garbed in the space-suit, but my weapon was gone. I was presently allowed to sit up in a chair beside Brenda and her father. But for all my assumption that I could be bribed, it did not deceive the wily Jerome. The two other black-garbed men here were closely watching me.

*

The Phantom flyer. From here in its tiny control room, it did not seem unusually weird. Its fittings a dead-black metal. Its men garbed in sleek, dead-black, close-fitting fabric suits with black fabric helmets dangling at the back of the neck.

I could see that we were in space. Through the pressure dome the stars were glittering in a black firmament. Where were we going? Jerome had not the slightest objection to telling me. Perhaps in the back of his mind there was the idea that ultimately he could bribe me, make me one of his band of cutthroats, useful to him. He was a genial, triumphant villain now, flushed with his success, pleased to boast of it before his men and before Brenda.

Old Professor Carson had not intended that his children come to Asteroid-9 and try to rescue him. That furtive message he had found opportunity to send was intended to bring the Interplanetary Police. Jerome had discovered that the message was sent. On the *Seven Stars* he had thrust Philip out through the porte; and had been searching Philip's stateroom, fearing that some incriminating evidence might be there, when I assailed him.

"You were using an X-ray screen?" he jibed at me now. "My metal headplate? Much good will it ever do you now to know that I was the Chameleon. A clever fellow, that Chameleon—but I like the Phantom bandit better, don't you?"

And then he told me gloatingly how easy it had been for him to don a pressure-suit and hide in the pressure-room while he wrecked the air-valves and let the air out of the doomed *Seven Stars*. Ship of the dead, on which he was the only living human until his phantom raider had come with a boarding party. Then the *Seven* had been taken to Asteroid-9, her cargo of electronic weapons transferred to the arriving X-flyer, and here we were.

"Headed for Deimos," he chuckled. "How glad they will be to see us! A million decimars of Interplanetary currency, Fanning. You'll want some of it, surely. And then we'll go looking for another adventure. Romantic life, eh?"

I tried, during those following hours, very cautiously to convince Jerome that at heart I might be a villain like himself. Perhaps to some extent, I succeeded. At all events, there came at last a brief interval when the controls were locked and Brenda, her father and I were out on the tiny forepeak in the starlight, momentarily alone. I had found now that a little freedom of movement was given us. After all, there was nothing that we could do, trapped here.

"You know where the exit porte of this ship is?" I murmured.

"Yes, yes, of course." Professor Carson was a confused, dazed old man; his life among these cutthroats for so long now had cowed him. "But what—what do you think you could do?"

In truth I had no possible idea. But if ever a chance should come for escape—

"In the pressure chamber," I whispered, "would there be pressure suits? One for you—"

"Yes. Yes, there are."

A commotion up at the control turret interrupted us. The black-garbed man at the electro-telescope there was shouting. Jerome came running; and we followed him up into the turret. He was grim, but ironically smiling.

"Interplanetary Patrolship off there," he said. "Patrolship-3."

Sister ship of my ill-fated vessel.

"Sighted us?" I murmured.

He shrugged. "Probably. Only three thousand miles away—probably did." His mouth was set into a grim hard line. In his eyes I saw that gleam of fanatic irrationality. "Unfortunate, for them. This little vessel of mine has never been sighted before, you know." His lips twitched with a grin. "You see how we are dressed here? Why, we've even been down into Earth's atmosphere—we've landed and made away without discovery. We'll do that on Deimos. And now this Patrolship—no one on it will ever live to tell that even for a moment they sighted the Phantom raider!"

He turned to an intricate bank of levers, dials and tiny vacuum globes that were ranged on a table here at the side of the control room. Separate from the space-flying mechanisms. The controls of the mechanical electronic invisibility.

"You'll see us go into action now, Fanning. It should be interesting."

He swung the dials. I felt my senses reel with a weird shock. Brenda gave a little gasp. There was a momentary quiver of all the ship; a momentary current-hum. And then silence.

My head cleared; the shock was passed. I gripped the arms of my chair and stared.

*

A glow like an aura of green radiance suffused the control room. A green glow of unreality throughout all the little ship. I could see it out on the forepeak triangle—the black-garbed figures like wraiths out there in a luminous green gloom. The glassite bull's-eye portes seemed now to have a green film on them. The stars outside were shut away. The transparent glassite dome was spread with the same dull-green opaqueness now. And then I saw, here in the turret walls, in the dome and in the center of each of the bull's-eyes, little holes through which a tiny segment of the starfield still was apparent—windows like dull little eyes puncturing our barrage of invisibility so that we could see outward through them.

Here in the control room the dull radience shone upon Jerome's grinning, triumphant face; it was tinted ghastly, putty-colored by the strange light. And the light glistened on his eyeballs, glowing like phosphorescence—like the eyes of an animal in a hunter's torchlight at night.

Everyone here, the same. And I saw old Professor Carson's face—the face of a dead man. His expression was stamped with his mixed emotions. This, his science of which he had been so proud, perverted now into murderous, ghastly warfare by the villainous Jerome.

Then Jerome moved to his space-flight controls; through the tiny windows in the barrage I could see that our ship was swinging, heading for the oncoming patrolship. Only three thousand miles apart. They would be upon each other in a few minutes.

Jerome's footsteps as he moved across the room faintly sounded on the metal floor-grid. Toneless footsteps in this eerie radiance. Unreal—they might have been tinkling bells, or harsh thuds. All timbre had gone from them so that they had lost their identity completely.

"Not long now, Fanning," Jerome said. "You'll see that ship go to its death." Ghastly dead voice. Every overtone had gone from it. It could have been a man's voice, or a woman's. The voice of a dead thing in a hollow tomb.

"Weird—" I muttered. My own voice the same. And Brenda's, as she murmured something in horror. All dead, indistinguishable one from the other.

Down on the forepeak in the sodden dull-green light, I could see the crew raising the electronic gun-carriages into position now. They were quite evidently of the most modern Edretch type, squat projectors with grid faces fitted into vacuum firing portes on each side of the forepeak. Guns undoubtedly with an effective range of some five hundred Earth-miles.

X-flyer going into action. The crew, with their dead putty-colored faces, moved, silently in the soundless ship. Up here in the turret with us, Jerome's hollow voice was gloating:

"That fool patrolship—they have seen us vanish. They know now who their adversary is. Want to see them, Fanning?"

There was no need of a telescope now. A magnified image of the oncoming patrolship as seen through one of the little barrage-vents on our bow, was spread here on a grid-screen in the control turret. Fascinated with horror, I watched it—the foreshortened looming bow of the patrolship clearly outlined against the black velvet of the firmament. It had seen us vanish, had turned and was heading straight for where it had last seen us! Even as I watched, the image of it was visibly enlarging. A thousand miles away now, probably. But almost in a moment it would be within range!

Then the wily Jerome abruptly swung us sharply. He was still at his gravity-control levers. The starfield rolled sidewise as we turned in a great hundred-mile arc. The maneuver was obvious. The patrolship had marked our position. Jerome quite evidently was not sure what range-guns his adversary had. He was taking no chances that a premature shot, aimed by calculation at where we might be, would strike us.

Patrolship-3 had guns very similar to these which I saw now being erected here on the X-flyer. It could have been a fairly even battle, a test of electronic battery-strength, of astronomical skill, of reckless daring—and yet, against an invisible enemy it could be no fight at all! I knew the commander of Patrolship-3 well. A stalwart, youngish fellow named Rollins. A man of infinite skill, reckless daring. I could picture him now in the turret of his ship, with his mouth set grim and his eyes flashing as he hurtled his little vessel forward. At what? Nothing but an apparently empty starfield from some unknown quarter of which a sudden stab of bolt would leap to strike him! I knew what Commander Rollins was thinking now. He would watch for that first bolt, and if it did not wreck his ship he would fire at the blankness from whence the shot had come. His only chance. An almost hopeless one. And yet he had done his best to hurl himself at us.

*

We were circling now. And suddenly it seemed that Rollins' ship, with its side spread toward us, off there at some five hundred miles, was slackening its velocity. Like a lion at bay, stopping, waiting with an invisible soundless wasp encircling it.

One of the gunners down in our forepeak signaled up to Jerome.

"Not yet," Jerome called. "When we strike, it must smash. There must not even be a chance of an answering shot."

Maneuvering for the kill. Fascinated, silently I watched as again we were heading for Rollins' ship. And within me a vague, desperate thought was growing: There are things through which one has no right to live. If only I could contrive it.

Jerome was absorbed at his controls, his range-finders and his calculations. My hand touched Brenda's arm where she sat beside me. I whispered:

"Brenda, we may not live through this."

"I know."

"I mean, if we were to die, to help that other ship."

She stared at me, and then at her father. Jerome had called the old man, ordered him to the mechanisms of the vessel's invisibility, where he sat checking the dial-readings of his intricate apparatus.

Briefly, its operation involved three scientific factors: De-electronization, thus to create around any metallic object a barrage of magnetic field of a new type to any previously developed; color-absorption, by which there can be no reflected light from the de-electronized object; and the Albert Einstein principle of the natural bending of light-rays when passing through a magnetic field. In effect then, the total color-absorption into the de-electronized object would make it, when viewed externally, a *nothingness* to see. A blankness, like an outlined dark hole. But that in itself is not invisibility—merely a silhouette. The background would be blotted out, so that the invisible object would be perceived by the background it obscured. The magnetic field, however, by natural law which Einstein discovered, bends the light-rays from the background, *around* the intervening object. The background thus seems complete. The intervening object has vanished!

Simple in theory; but it was an intricate little apparatus here which now old Professor Carson was attending. I stared at him as he bent so earnestly over it. His beloved brain-child.

For that moment Brenda tenderly regarded him. And then she turned to me. Her eyes were misted.

"Whatever you think best," she murmured.

Tensely I was waiting my chance. That tiny row of fragile vacuum tubes.

My heart pounded suddenly as Jerome locked his space-controls and darted down to the forepeak to consult one of his men at a gun-range finder. I muttered:

"Brenda take your father and get out of here quickly!" A burly, black-garbed guard was coming in from the turret balcony to watch us in Jerome's absence. I added in a swift undertone: "Go down with Jerome. Find some pretense to help him."

They would escape Jerome's wrath and there was just a chance that they might live through this.

They had only reached the little balcony outside the turret when the guard came in. I was on my feet.

"Sit down," he commanded.

He was between me and the little table where Carson's tiny row of vacuum tubes glowed dull-green. And in that second I leaped, head down like a battering ram. With my skull striking his middle he went backward, spun as he tried to get his balance. And he landed, sprawled forward on Carson's little table.

There was a tinkling crash as the de-electronizers short-circuited. A hiss of neutronic flame which in that second with its half-million ultra-pressure oscillating volts, electrocuted the luckless villain who was sprawled there.

I was down on the floor, crawling in the chaos. Amazing, electronic turmoil. The shock of it swiftly spread around the little vessel; made the senses of everyone on board momentarily reel. I was aware of thin slivers of neutronic fire darting upward from the cooking flesh of the sprawling man's body. Neutronic fire that all in that second of deranged current darted throughout the ship. A split second of flash; but in that second the darting tiny slivers of light-fire everywhere were drinking up the weird green glow. The muffled ghastly, toneless sounds of the ship's interior were brought to life. Down on the forepeak Jerome gasped a startled curse. One of his men fell with reeling senses.

And light was here. Normal celestial light, streaming down through our transparent dome where the blazing firmament of stars was now clearly to be seen. We had lost our invisibility! Gone. Irrevocably gone. At least this combat would be upon an equality! Rollins at last had his equal chance with the Phantom raider!

Patrolship-3 was clearly apparent now through our forward dome. I saw Rollins swing his bow toward us. There was a tiny violet flash from his forepeak. The first shot!

It came like a great violet lightning bolt hurtling at us!

*

There was a puff of electronic light up at our dome-peak. A shower of red-yellow sparks. I held my breath as Rollins' little circle of violet beam struck us full, and clung. A second. Ten seconds, while the shower of sparks sprayed like a little fountain of light-points. Would the outer shell of our dome crack?

It seemed to hold. Ten seconds, and then Rollins' ray snapped off and vanished. A test shot. I knew it was not a weakness of his electronic power. A great, long-range space-gun with a single snap-bolt ordinarily can do little damage. It is the duration of seconds over which the bolt can cling, eating its way with generated interference-heat, fusing and breaking its opposing armored substance.

And this was Rollins' first tentative test. Verifying his range, and our ship's resistance. A conservation of his electronic power. In space-gun battle, the available reserve of battery strength is vital. A long-range gun, with ten seconds of sustained voltage, drains any battery-series faster than the whirling electro-dynamos can build them up. Then there must be an interval of replenishment.

My heart pounded with exultation as the thoughts swept me. Rollins had been grimly desperate, undoubtedly, against an invisible enemy. But his adversary was visible now. An equality of battle; and so Rollins would use his wits, his skill of judgment. This damned murderous Jerome would have all he could do to match tactics with the skilful commander of Patrolship-3!

In those chaotic seconds I was still on the floor near the door of the control room. Inside it the dead, roasted body of my guard lay sprawled face down upon the wreckage of the invisibility-controls. The current there was shut off now. The slivers of light-fire were gone. Down on our forepeak Jerome and his gunners were recovering. Jerome was gazing up, wildly cursing.

I staggered to the little turret-balcony, where Brenda and her father, white-faced, were clinging to its rail.

"That damned fool!" I shouted. "In there—in the turret. He stumbled and fell on the control table."

Would it serve as an excuse? Would the raging Jerome stab at me now with a heat-bolt? Or would he believe me? I felt sure that no one actually had seen what had happened.

"You damned—why—why—" Jerome for that instant glared up at me, his hand instinctively reaching for his belt. But in all the chaos, turning his wrath upon me must have struck him as futile. And it was stricken from his mind by the confusion around him. Acrid choking fumes were swirling through our little vessel, fumes from the deranged current of the de-electronizers. One of Jerome's men dashed up to him.

"A fire on our stern-deck. I put it out."

"Go back to your post." Jerome shoved him away impatiently; turned, came up and went into his turret, and seated himself at his gravity controls.

Through the dome-peak I could see Rollins' ship, going in the opposite direction from us, hurtling past us. Two hundred miles off. In a moment it had passed and was out of range. Then it was turning, mounting in a great arc and hurtling back at us!

*

Jerome stabbed first. A hit! The violet sword dimly glowing, luminous as it ignited the motes of intervening star-dust, leaped across the narrowing angle and struck with a puff of glare. Jerome held it, clinging. Five seconds. Ten. Fifteen. I could hear the throb and whir of our dynamos as they struggled with the load. The big dial levers on Jerome's desk quivered, slowly turned backward toward zero as our batteries drained.

For those seconds Rollins took it with no answering shot. Would his forepeak dome hold? I could see the tiny puff of fountain-light there where the violet beam was boring. And then Rollins answered! From his stern-peak this time diagonally away from us, his beam shot out. Not directly at us, but at our bolt-stream. Two great violet rapiers in space, sliding one upon the other. Midway between the vessels they clashed. The interference cut our beam from Rollins' vessel. Out there in space for breathless seconds both the beams held firm. Amazing sight of pyrotechnic beauty, that area where the beams clashed.

Another ten seconds, each of them an eternity. The giant circle of the interference area slowly was backing toward Rollins' ship! Our beam, at reckless full-power now, was pushing it back. Only twenty or thirty miles now from its target.

A buzzer sounded at Jerome's elbow. He reached for his audiphone. The panic-stricken voice of our controlman in the ship's hull sounded:

"Chief! Dynamo bearing running hot! An' we're almost at zero in the main battery."

Jerome disconnected with a grim curse. Another few seconds. The narrowing angle of the hurtling ships had brought them within a hundred miles of each other. And then suddenly, again it was Rollins who was the more cautious. From the tail of his vessel a stream of burning gas suddenly was issuing. A widening fluorescent comet-tail streaming out behind him. And then he was turning, heading away from us! In retreat! The interference area of the two clashing sword-beams broke. The great prismatic spark shower died. Our bolt, plunging through, for a second may have struck the turning, retreating Rollins. No one here could say. Rollins' bolt had snapped off. The image of his ship merged with the gas cloud. Vanished behind its masking cloak.

Jerome snapped off our beam. His face was triumphant; his enemy fleeing, trying to mask his retreat with a cloud of burning gas.

"By Heaven, I've got him!" Jerome was muttering. "Damn' fool, trying to fight the Phantom."

The starfield swung as we turned, headed at the gas-cloud where it hung in a vast luminous fog of prismatic color as though a comet had burst there. Triumphant pursuit of our enemy. But I held my breath.

I found Brenda beside me. Her hand, cold dank, gripped mine. Our eyes met. There was nothing to say. Surely we both knew what little chance we had of coming out of this alive.

The luminous gas-cloud swarmed to the sides as our ship plunged headlong into it. And then we were through it.

*

There was no warning as Rollins' bolt struck us! He had not tried to escape but was poised here in ambush, bow toward us, no more than fifty miles away, off to one side by skilled calculation so that there was only his narrow bow as our target and we were almost broadside to him!

The bolt struck us midway of the hull in a shower of sparks that mounted up and clouded our instruments. Clinging, full-power beam. Rollins at last striking for the kill! Wildly our guns tried to intercept it. One of our forepeak guns went out of commission with a back-firing burst which shattered it and killed the man at its controls. The fumes of the explosion came wafting up, acrid, choking.

There was a sudden panic of confusion here, but Jerome leaped to his feet with his roaring voice steadying his men. Then two of our guns, stem and bow, stabbed beams that struck the patrolship's bow and clung. But still that blast at our hull persisted. Eating, fusing the metallic hull-plate.

Weird, transfixed drama as the seconds passed. I knew that Rollins now would never yield. This bolt would cling to the limit of his batteries.

The audiphone beside Jerome was screaming with the hull-controlman's panic-stricken voice: "Chief—hull plate is bending—bulging—"

Then I saw, through the shower of sparks outside, that Rollins' ship was edging even closer. One of our two bolts had wavered and broken, with exhausted battery. The other, weakened by all Jerome's reckless firing, was futilely clinging to its target with a shower of sparks paling now by diminished voltage.

And then from the patrolship, little blobs were popping out. Catapulted bombs, hurtling at us with this close, twenty-mile range. Some exploded in mid-space fired by the free electrons which hung heavy here around us. And then one struck us, exploded with a dull concussion against our stern. And then another, and another.

"Jim—Jim dear—goodbye."

Brenda's murmured words brought me suddenly to myself. Only sixty seconds had passed since we burst out of the gas-cloud and Rollins had jumped to finish us. Sixty seconds, but it had brought chaos here on the Phantom ship. My chance! Old Professor Carson beside us was in a daze; white-faced, numbly staring.

"The exit-porte," I muttered. "Brenda, make your father hurry."

Fumes of green-yellow chlorine mingled with oil-smoke, were surging around us as we staggered up the little catwalk from the balcony to the dome-top. Jerome may have seen us. His voice was shouting desperate orders, and curses, but whether at us or not I never knew. A gunner down on the deck fired at us with a hand-ray, but it missed.

"Brenda, hurry! Get your father into a space-suit."

She and I still were garbed in the space-suits from the *Seven Stars*. In the tiny exit-porte, one of Jerome's crew, himself trying to escape, lunged at me, but I felled him with a blow of my fist into his face. The closing slide-door of the tiny pressure chamber shut away the chaos. Then our suits were inflated; our helmets fixed and we catapulted into the glare of outside space. I flung on my rocket-stream; clung to Brenda and her father. My metal-tipped fingers on the metallic plate of her shoulder made audiphone contact.

"Hold tight, Brenda."

"Yes, Jim."

"I'll tow us."

Horrible, chaotic seconds as the showering electronic sparks from the doomed phantom flyer enveloped us. Indescribable glaring confusion of deranged electricity and fusing, bubbling, flying metal-fragments. Prismatic light that blinded.

We came through it in a moment, out into the starlight with the glaring, staggering vessel, receding behind and above us as my rocket-stream and gravity-plates drew us out of the line of fire. The patrolship was hardly ten miles away now. I signalled with a helmet-flare. Interplanetary Code signal. Rollins saw it; recognized it; answered it!

We hurtled forward. Behind us, well overhead now, Jerome's harried, wavering ship suddenly cracked. With a great burst of interior pressure the dome, to which Rollins' main beam had shifted, abruptly exploded outward. Ghastly, silent explosion. It spewed wreckage. Little hurtling dots of shattered glassite and metal and mangled humans—blobs that spewed out, were caught by the vessel's attraction, finding their orbits so that they circled, gruesome satellites of their convulsed world.

Then the last of Rollins' blasting beams snapped off. Back there the broken ship hung leprous, with fused, still bubbling dome. Like a bent finger of colored light for a moment more it glowed. And then it went dark.

Dead X-flyer among the stars. The end of the dreaded Phantom of the Starways.